I0592642

MONROVIA

Rain

AND OTHER STORIES

LOST AND
FOUND

MONROVIA

AND OTHER STORIES

LOST AND FOUND

EDITED BY ELMA SHAW

cottonTree
Press

MONROVIA RAIN AND OTHER STORIES
LOST AND FOUND
Copyright © 2018 by Cotton Tree Press

Authors retain the copyright for their individual stories.

Vamba Sherif's photo by Chris van Houts
All other author photos by Edana Photography

Homecoming, by Vamba Sherif, was first published in the One World Two anthology (New Internationalist, 2016)

First Cotton Tree Press edition: September 2018

Published by Cotton Tree Press
Washington DC
Monrovia, Liberia
www.ctpbooks.com

ISBN: 978-0-9800774-9-0
eISBN: 978-1-7326795-0-4

Library of Congress Control Number: 2018956961

Printed in the United States of America

To order discounted copies of *Monrovia Rain and Other Stories Lost and Found* in bulk for your school, charity or organization, or to arrange a speaking engagement with one of our authors, please write to cottontreepress@gmail.com. All titles by Cotton Tree Press can also be found at African Books Collective.

Book layout by Velin Saramov

For those who understand that though we may not live in the past, the past lives in us.

Contents

Monrovia Rain
by Augustus Y. Voahn

There he was in the rain, soaked, drenched and cold to the bone. He was laughing and crying too. Water dripping all over him, from his hair and rolling down. Tears rolling down the eyes, slimy liquid running down the nostrils. But why was he laughing? Because suffering has been his way of life. Laughing the only way to keep himself alive.

[Page 35]

Another Dead Girl
by Gii-Hne S. Russell

In the meantime, she pondered over the fortune that had befallen her. She could still scarcely believe that it was real. It was like a dream too grand to be true! All her problems were over now.

[Page 55]

Homecoming
by Vamba Sherif

We loaded the jeep with bags of rice and other foodstuffs for the family in Wologizi. By the time the city awoke, we were far beyond its borders. The driver was good. I marveled at how he skillfully avoided the potholes that littered the roads and, when I commented on this, he said without hesitation or shame, "I was a driver for a rebel faction during the war."

[Page 65]

Introduction

The authors featured in *Monrovia Rain and Other Stories Lost and Found* are not brand new to the literary world. Between the four of them, they have published children's books, poems, and novels that have been critically acclaimed. All of them, however, are relatively new when it comes to contemporary short stories, and their voices in this arena are as diverse and interesting as their backgrounds and experiences.

In this anthology you will find five very different stories, all with a common theme: the effect of war on the psyche, and on a nation as a whole. This was not the plan. When we first put out a call for submissions, we were hoping for stories about all aspects of life in Liberia. When the stories came in, we asked, bewildered: *Is the war all we can think about? And where are the female voices?* Not a single woman submitted a story. We selected the best of what came in, and worked with the authors to get their stories ready for publication. In the meantime we put out more calls, and waited, in vain, for more stories. At some point we considered abandoning the project, but then a friend, himself a Liberian author, reminded us that although the war was over, it would be at the forefront of our thoughts and imaginations for a long while. He was right. In fact, it's difficult to lay down the burden of war when the reasons you are carrying it have yet to be adequately addressed. Transitional justice comes in many forms, and we can't continue to ignore them all or to approach national healing half-heartedly.

Each author featured in these pages loves storytelling not only for entertainment, but also for a greater purpose. In personal narratives that describe the thinking and feeling behind the stories they chose to share, you will get to know them better and gain insights into the complicated landscape of which they write. Through Gii-Hne Russell's intense portrayal of his main characters, and Augustus Voahn's uniquely expressed observations, you will be transported to intimate places and emotions not often laid bare for all to see. Woryonwon Roberts addresses crime and punishment from new perspectives that give us food for thought, while Vamba Sherif's beautiful semi-autobiographical story invites the reader to consider the important role of memory—of both the good things and the bad.

Memories of the war live on, and always will, but so do memories of good times. Different narratives and female voices are emerging in different forms, and I'm excited to see what the future will bring. *Monrovia Rain and Other Stories*, lost for a while, but thankfully found again, is a testament to the talent present and waiting to bloom despite hardships and obstacles of every kind.

I would like to thank everyone who helped in some way to bring this anthology to life, especially those who encouraged us to keep the dream alive, and the readers who provided valuable feedback on each story. Most of all, I'd like to thank the authors who responded to the call for submissions and demonstrated extraordinary patience as we worked to bring their stories to you.

Elma Shaw
September 2018

The Last Flight
Gii-Hne S. Russell

Wilson, big and tall, and very worried, walked about the house aimlessly. A safari shirt and a pair of shorts and sandals was all he wore. It was a contrast to the immaculately attired and smiling picture of him on the wall. As though the picture angered him, he rushed to it and took down. He tore it out of its frame and put it in a folder that he had taken from one of the bags that were scattered about the piazza. He stuffed the folder back into the bag and slummed into one of the sofas. But his bottom had barely landed when he flew to his feet again. Someone was coming to the front door. He rushed to the door and opened it. His shoulders sagged. He rolled his eyes upward and lifted his leg to stamp his foot but checked himself just in time.

"How do," the woman said, already looking discouraged, sure that she had come in vain. She was a little old woman. Her face was lined with wrinkles due more to shrinking caused by starvation than to age. Her clothes hung loose on her and her head-tie was askew.

"Hello Ma," Wilson replied.

The woman hesitated. Wilson's reply and changed expression encouraged her. "My son, I've come to beg you. Since last night..."

"Wait, I'm coming," Wilson said impatiently as he snatched the plastic bag from the woman's hand. He rushed to the master bedroom. His wife Lucy was there on the bed with two of their children, a four-year-old girl and a nine-year-old boy, both sitting on her lap. Lucy looked up eagerly when Wilson entered, as if she expected some news. Ignoring her, Wilson went to the corner where a big barrel stood.

"Some old lady out there," was all he said as he delved in the sack of rice. Then he reached into the box filled with canned food. He picked random cans and filled the old woman's bag.

"Wilson," Lucy moaned as she watched him.

Wilson thrust the bag into the arms of the elated woman and closed the door before she could shower him with gratitude. He went to the sofa again and this time the landing of his bottom heralded a fierce firing from the Sinkor area. Wilson's innards turned into a tight spiny ball that pricked him. The firing brought an uneasiness that eroded every thought of trying to relax. "If only they could do their fighting somewhere else," he groaned. He went to one of the windows. Pulling the curtains aside, he peeked down on central Monrovia, which was mainly deserted except for army vehicles crossing the intersections occasionally.

The firing went on as though it was the final battle to decide the war. Then, after thirty minutes, it stopped abruptly. Wilson went to check on his family. Lucy looked up again but not with as much expectation as before. She bowed her head dismally. Wilson wanted to talk to her. He really wanted to comfort her and the children but he didn't have the spirit. He was unable to be the husband and father he once was. Wilson only patted the children on their heads after which he went out hurriedly. In the next room was his thirteen-year-old son, his 'junior boy'. The boy lay on his bed completely engrossed in the comic book he was reading. He didn't look up until Wilson stood right over him.

Two things came to Wilson's mind. The first was to give the boy a hard lecture. Here they were in the middle of a nightmare and the stupid boy was reading comics. The second was to borrow, if possible, the boy's serenity, his assured calmness amid the precarious time in which they were living. He drew closer to the bed.

"Papa," the boy said.

"You're enjoying your story?"

"Yeah," the boy said wearily as he gathered himself. But Wilson stopped him.

"Enjoy your book son," Wilson said before he left.

Something told Wilson not to sit again, but he did anyway. This time, an outburst of explosions, followed by another fierce round of firing, erupted around the Freeport area. "Oh God," Wilson whined like a sick dog. He raised his arms sorrowfully and looked up to the ceiling, a man beseeching God. He quickly desisted when he heard someone coming down the hall, and the petition he had in mind was not said.

It was Lucy. She pulled up the trousers she wore when she got into the piazza. No worry showed in her face, only a tight frown. Lucy never wore trousers. It was one of Wilson's trousers that she had on. Looking at her made Wilson nervous. He was reminded of Dehconti, the wife of Joe Benson, his boyhood buddy. Whenever Dehconti wore trousers like that it meant business, serious fighting business that he was often called to settle. It didn't cross his mind that Lucy had put on the trousers due to the pending trip and the tension under which the trip was to be taken. Wilson got up to leave.

"And where do you think you are going?" Lucy asked with a scowl. Wilson clutched his groin and pointed to the hall, indicating he wanted to pee. "Sit down man," Lucy said. She blocked his way. "Look Wilson, let me tell you: you will be responsible if anything happens to me and my children."

"Ay Lucy, please. Nothing will happen. Jallah will come and we will go."

"Where? When will Jallah come? You are too damn hard to hear. We should have vacated this damn country ever since but you won't listen. You are the kind of person who will not pay attention

8

until the one warning you about a snake is forced to put his finger on it and get bitten. People were being slaughtered on our left and right everyday, things were deteriorating day by day but you still wouldn't listen to my plea for us to leave."

"Lucy, please be patient."

"Patient? Are you going to take me and my children patiently to our graves? How will the plane leave in this fighting? What if it's being shot at by the rebels right now? Even if Jallah manages to get through this fighting, how do you know that the rebels won't seize the money from him? In fact, who would be foolish enough to risk his life by going through this terrible fighting for any reason?"

"Let's be optimistic Lucy."

"To hell with your optimism Wilson!" Lucy blazed. "It's your greed that has gotten us trapped here today."

"Where are these insults coming from, Lucy?"

"From your inability to look after your family! You put money and possessions before me and the children. You could have even allowed us to leave while you stayed behind to protect your company, but you refused. You went on lending money to your friends who were leaving while you sat here doing nothing. Now we've got no money, and where is your company now?"

"Lucy stop it, please stop it," Wilson said.

Lucy's hand shot out in a flash and Wilson felt a sharp pain in his left jaw. It was not so much the slap that hurt, but that the timid Lucy had resorted to violence. Wilson stared at her. She swallowed and stared back defiantly, inviting him to hit her so she could vent the agitation that had been in her once and for all. *What will it solve?* Wilson thought. "Do you know what Lucy? I won't hit you back."

"You aren't even a fool to do it," Lucy retorted. "I dare you to hit me."

She really wants to fight, Wilson thought. "I'm not a fool to hit you." Wilson's voice was calm but his face was harsh. "All I can say is go to the room, fall on your knees, and pray. Pray Lucy, that God lets the rebels kill Jallah, and pray that they steal the money from him. Pray that God directs one of the rockets to hit the plane and set it ablaze. Then pray finally that a bomb should fall on our house and destroy us all."

"You idiot!" Lucy shrieked. "You wicked fool! That's what you wanted all along isn't it? You sat with your hands between your thighs while your friends fled with their families, and…"

"Yes, that is why," Wilson interrupted.

"And everyday you keep sharing the food I have stored to sustain us!" Lucy finished.

"I want us to starve," Wilson said as he walked away, for it was obvious that Lucy could get more violent.

"What is it now Papa?" the boy asked as he came from his room. The younger children stood at their parents' room door, staring.

"Why is this woman bugging me?" Wilson responded to the boy.

Lucy kept railing, this time in tears, making the other children cry. Wilson was heading for the bathroom when he remembered he didn't really want to pee. He changed direction and went to the kitchen instead. Lucy went to the children and gathered them into her arms. "Let's go my children," she said. "God will make a way. He's the only one who will protect us." She entered the room, and the boy followed her.

Through the open door, Wilson could hear the boy consoling his mother and siblings. The shooting at Freeport had stopped. Wilson stood staring out of the kitchen window with his hands in his pockets, trying to get over what had happened. He turned when he heard the door squeak. It was the boy.

"We're in this horrible civil war and you are quarreling with Mama?" the boy asked. "Are you bringing one more civil war in our home?" Wilson searched his son's face as if the boy was not serious. Was the boy taking sides with his mother? But the boy came closer. "Maybe Mama is right. You had the money to take us away. I thought we were going to leave with the Freemans, but they left and we stayed. Mama is afraid. You are not supposed to quarrel with her."

"Look son, I'm sorry," Wilson said. "I admit that I made a great mistake by not getting us out of here. Right now I'm very anxious for us to leave. Your mother's nagging got me angry. If only I had known, if only I had known…" Wilson searched for the right things to say but found none. "We've got to get out of here."

"Just go and apologize to Mama," the boy said.

Such a change of roles! He's telling me what to do, and with authority! Wilson went to the master bedroom. Lucy sat staring out the window with the youngest child on her lap, tearstains still on her face. Wilson lifted the other child and set him on his lap as he sat by Lucy. She tried to get up but he held her back.

"Honey I'm sorry," he said. "I'm so sorry. You got best. All you said about me being insensitive to the sufferings around us and not leaving is true. I am to blame for getting us into this. I'm so sorry." Lucy leaned her head on his shoulder. "Jallah is our only hope," Wilson continued. "The plane leaves today and it will be the last for only God knows how long. Let's pray that Jallah comes. I don't know what to do if he doesn't come."

Wilson was on the piazza again, wearing a hole in the rug. His tension now was too palpable for him to be still. That he didn't know what to do if Jallah didn't come with the money was the truth. The indictment from his son only made him feel even guiltier. What he had seen the last time he ventured out proved that Monrovia was a hell. He tried not to regret. It only made things worse. Reaching the wall, he turned around to traverse to another point when he heard something outside. He rushed to the door and threw it open.

The spectacle that met Wilson's eyes sent his blood pressure escalating. He had to lean on the doorframe to steady himself. He peered closely. It was Jallah. Tattered short trousers, a pair of unmatched rubber slippers, shirt unevenly buttoned, hair unkempt and mud-spattered. One word summed him up: mad. He was startled by every trifling sound. His face bore the look of a man who had literally had a fight with death and survived, not because he had won but because he had been allowed to go so that he could die another day. Wilson's heart fell. Where he found the strength to leave the door and move down the steps, he didn't know.

Jallah stopped when he saw Wilson. He opened his arms as if for a hug and opened his mouth wide and continued walking. Wilson thought the man was going to erupt into wailing. Wilson fought back tears. *I'm a fool!* he thought. *I should have gotten my family out of here.* He walked to Jallah.

"Jallah, you are here," Wilson heard himself say.

Jallah exploded. "Wilson! Oh Wilson!"

Wilson really had to fight back his tears.

"Wilson! Liberia is finished!" Jallah shook his head emphatically. "There is no more Liberia, Wilson. No more." Jallah made pathetic gestures as he went on. "God is destroying us. We are destroyed. Tell me Wilson, what have we done? See children, and I mean small boys, talking about killing human beings as if they are talking about chickens. Wilson, see human beings lying everywhere rotting like rats! Oh God! Wilson, see people starving to death! See dogs eating dead human bodies and the rebels chasing those same dogs to eat them. Wilson my brother, we are finished. The rebels are everywhere killing people. I mean just like…guns, guns and guns my brother!"

Wilson hung his head as the man went on, unaware that his family was watching. He opened his mouth every now and then to say something but Jallah went on nonstop.

"Look!" Jallah turned as he took off his torn shirt. There was a long swath of bruises across his back. "See? This was done by one of those boys wielding a cutlass. Can you imagine? Those blood-thirsty boys tore up my shirt and one of them slapped me with the flat of his cutlass. Those boys wanted to butcher me! Boys that in normal days I could put kicks in their butts and they will shit blood!" Jallah turned around again. "The mark here on my chest was made by another rebel who pricked me with his dagger. They stripped me naked. They took my sneakers too. I just found these rags and this dirt," he kicked the slippers off his feet, "by the road. Let the Americans just bomb this damn country so that everybody can die!"

Jallah finally noticed Wilson's family. "Don't even think about this stupid country again when you leave with your family," he said.

"Leave?" Wilson followed Jallah's eyes and turned to see his family at the door. He turned back to Jallah angrily and threw up his arms. "How the hell do you expect me to get my family out of this hell if the money you…"

"Oh, the money!" Jallah said. "I forgot…"

Wilson watched with his mouth ajar as the man fumbled with his dirty shorts. Now he was convinced that whatever ordeal Jallah had gone through that morning had left him mad.

"Oh?" Jallah said after digging into the first pocket. Then he dug into the second one. "Oh?" He checked his hip pockets. "Oh? Ah, I'm forgetting." Jallah unzipped his shorts and reached into his under pants. He pulled out a small plastic-wrapped bundle of clean US dollars tightly rolled up.

This time Wilson could not hold back his tears. "Oh Jallah!" he said rushing at Jallah. "You could have killed me! You've brought the money and you had me waiting…!"

"Yeah," Jallah said. "The rebels stopped short of stripping me buck-naked. They would have killed me on the spot had they seen the money. I tell you Wilson, the rebels can kill you if they don't like the color of your clothes."

Jallah would have continued his lamentation but Wilson stopped him.

"Come Jallah," Wilson said, dragging him to the house. "Come change those rags." He waved the money triumphantly to his family. "We are leaving now."

Wilson let Jallah rest. The ordeal he had been through had left him on the brink of insanity. But after a sumptuous meal Jallah was a little bit back to himself, although trauma was still in his face. He said Wilson was carrying too much baggage. Only the essential things, he said, should be taken. He loaded the car trunk with food, which he said would help at the army checkpoints. All on board, Wilson was about to start the car when Lucy stopped him.

"Let's pray first," Lucy said.

"Yes," Wilson agreed.

To their blessing, there was not a single incident at any of the army checkpoints. The last remnant of the food was exhausted at the checkpoint before the airport, and when they arrived at the airport, everything went smoothly.

Wilson took Jallah aside. "Jallah," he said. "Why can't you come with us? I can make a way for the people to take you."

"No, Wilson," Jallah murmured. "You go with your family. I will find a way to leave or wait yet. I don't know if we will ever see each other again…"

"Alright, Jallah," Wilson said. "Thank you for risking your life just for me. Take charge of my property, my friend."

Soon, Wilson was seated in the plane. But again he felt that spiny knob in his innards and he grew tense. There was firing far away near Paynesville. Waiting was torturous for him as all sorts of worrisome thoughts raced through his mind. But all the ills and anxieties were left behind when the plane took off. Some people, including Lucy, clapped their hands, while other cried. Someone suggested the National Anthem and soon everybody, including Wilson's four-year-old daughter, was hailing Liberia.

Wilson looked about the plane and was aware that most of the passengers were renowned Liberians. They included politicians, businessmen and women, activists, professors, and ministers. Right behind him was Henry Andrews. The old man was gazing out of the window but Wilson could tell that his attention was not on the beautiful scene below. There was a notebook on Mr. Andrews' lap and a pen between his fingers. He seemed to have been writing a poem. Wilson stretched for a peek. The words he caught were:

Cry Liberia, cry
The world is watching while you die

Wilson suddenly felt sad, especially when Jallah's question re-echoed in his head: "What will become of Liberia?"

Gii-Hne S. Russell

Most of my stories come from listening to people. Since I started writing, my eyes and my ears are sharp for stories. I'm looking and listening for them at work, at home, when riding in taxis and buses, and when I'm at any gathering.

The Last Flight comes from the experience of my boss, who is also my mentor. He is a good 'lecturer' and whenever he is telling interesting stories he says to me, 'You can write this story!' *The Last Flight* was also influenced by the book *Cry Liberia, Cry*, by the late Henry Andrews. I like that book, especially the diary entries. In it, the author talks about a plane that came to Monrovia when rebels were attacking the city. I imagined that plane was the last plane and linked it with my boss's story.

When I wrote the first draft of *The Last Flight*, I was still a boy in Bong Mines. That was where the German-owned Bong Mining Company was based. We used to watch the mayhem and suffering in Monrovia on international television stations. Displaced people from Monrovia and other areas had the look of Alice in Wonderland when they got to Bong Mines because we still had food, running water, and electricity. We *did* have rebels in Bong Mines, and they were killing those they targeted, but the place was not a war zone where people were starving to death or being slaughtered wholesale. Though there was no fighting at the time, the rebels were everywhere with their guns and their cars decorated with human skulls. They could brand you as President Doe's supporter, or a member of a tribe they were targeting. Or someone who you had some small issues with before the war could just pop up with a gun and decide that it was time that you die.

I was not thinking about a message when I wrote the story. But what comes to my mind when I look at the whole story is the effect of procrastination. Wilson had the means to get his family out of the country but delayed until the situation got worse and then had to hang his hope on his friend Jallah. Many people died during the war due to the 'wait and see' thing. It happens not only in time of war, but also with other adversities. We sometimes wait to see how things will go, or ignore warnings altogether until it is too late.

Time flies and people forget. You hear people making all sorts of threats of violence, especially around election time. But the Liberian people don't want to go back to such a terrible period of our history. People don't want to see all they have worked for be destroyed. This is why the Sirleaf government was careful not to do those things that led people to take up arms. This is why those who call for violence today are vehemently condemned. *The Last Flight* is a reminder to us of what we went through for almost a decade and a half.

Between Crimes

M. Woryonwon Roberts

The pandemic Christmas fever was prevailing once again. It was December 2002, and the twenty-fifth was nearing day by day. Somah took a panoramic view of Broad Street when he disembarked from the taxicab. It was a hot and humid Thursday afternoon and he was caught in its heat. The cab had taken him from the diplomatic enclave of Mamba Point where he had had an appointment. He walked briskly across the street and stopped before the Education Plaza. He hesitated for a moment and then made up his mind to stroll down to Waterside and board a bus for home. Waterside, especially at this time of the year, was like a colony of driver ants: people bustling to buy the latest Christmas wares at the lowest prices possible. Season vendors who clogged the streets went shouting, some even clinking silver bells, as they advertised their auction goods. It was as if all the people of Monrovia and its suburban areas had congregated there.

Somah had barely reached Waterside, by way of Mechlin Street, when he met an angry mob beating a man.

"He's a rogue!"

"He jerked the woman's handbag."

"A rogue? But he should be dead!"

"Where's the thief? Where? Where?"

"Let's finish him off quick!"

Slaps. Kicks. Blows. All laced with insults. They flew from everywhere. Somah stood by and watched the scene from a safe distance. He was hooked. So hooked he could hardly budge from where he was standing. The crowd was swelling quickly: a string of pupils, a horde of peddlers, a sprinkling of car loaders and pickpockets, a crop of onlookers and sympathizers. They were all shouting and damning and throwing objects at the disheveled middle-aged man. On the man's face a steady trickle of blood streamed from a deep cut on his temple.

Somah watched, unmindful now of the sweltering heat and the foul odor that was coming from an overstayed heap of garbage nearby. But with every fleeting second he became more and more conscious of the murderous, explosive nature of the crowd that would eventually spell the suspect's doom. *The war has made Liberians uncompromisingly wicked and violent*, he thought. The whole country was weary of war but the repercussions of the war—especially the culture of vengeance—were flames too strong to quench. The faces of the people held the bitterness, frustrations and hardships of the years spent fighting a needless civil war.

Some people held firmly to the battered man, while another batch rocked him every now and then with kicks, slaps and blows. Standing by the man was a young lady, in her early twenties, who was crying uncontrollably. Her right hand held tight onto the loose end of the man's clothes while her other hand clung to a bulging black plastic bag. Her eyes were red from crying.

"You must bring back my bag, you rogue!" the victim shouted in a hoarse, outraged voice. The suspect had no chance to talk back. Many hands were close on him. He tried to protest his innocence, but hands rose up to slap him again and again. Two women, with tired and worn features, spat at his face.

"You better give us the woman's bag. If not, we will skin you alive," a man from the crowd shouted, displaying a long knife from the pile he was selling.

"Let's take him to the police station," somebody suggested.

"No! No! No!" several others from the crowd objected.

"Let's just burn him."

"Or skin him."

"No! Beat him to death!"

"Yes! That's true. We don't need to take him anywhere. Let's just finish him off right here, right now!" a lanky fellow waving a box of matches said. He immediately struck a match and held it up for everyone to see. Then he took a piece of plastic and burned it close to the suspect's face and said, "That's how we will see you burn any moment from now." The crowd broke into laughter and cheers of approval. "Somebody please get us kerosene or gas!" the lanky fellow called out.

"If you don't talk the truth now, your end is just a matter of seconds away," somebody else said.

"Please let him bring my bag back first before you kill him," the young lady said as she tightened her grip on the suspect.

"They're not tired frustrating people yet," a woman with a basket of assorted fruits remarked. "They've killed and looted and still they're not satisfied."

"Old rebel! He's an old rebel!"

"The war has been over ever since but they don't want to find something better to do. They still want easy life, short cut."

"Let's do the man's work before the police come and spoil the show."

This last chilling remark brought a pang of sorrow to Somah's heart. That was the way of the rebels during the course of the war. Whenever they declared that a person's work was to be done, that person usually did not survive.

Now Somah felt compelled to intervene. He stepped forward and tried to get the crowd's attention. "Please, please, everybody!" He clapped his hands for silence. "Please listen!" Suddenly, as if under

24

a spell, the crowd became as quiet and attentive as it was noisy. Somah turned to those holding the suspect and said, "Please release his arms."

Grudgingly, the man was let alone. With his hands now free, he used the sleeve of his right arm to wipe away the blood from his face. Besides the deep cut on his head, the man's lips were swollen, his eyes were bloodshot and the eyelids puffy. He rearranged his torn shirt as best as he could as he looked at the crowd from behind half-closed eyes.

"Where's the woman's handbag? Why did you jerk it from her, in fact?" Somah asked.

"No sir. Not me. I know nothing about her bag," the suspect said. "I swear to God, I can't steal. I didn't jerk any bag."

"You're lying! You jerked my handbag. You can lie and steal and kill. You're a rogue!" the aggrieved woman shouted as loudly as she could.

"Talk the truth. You'll be set free. Where is the bag?" Somah tried to coax the embattled man.

"I swear I don't know about her bag."

Turning to the woman, Somah inquired, "Are you sure this is the man who snatched your handbag?"

"Yes I am. I'm more than sure. He is the one. He jerked the bag from me and gave it to another person who ran away with it."

"You saw me jerking your bag?" the suspect argued. "Oh God, my bad luck!"

"Do I want to lie on you? To gain what? I'm not stupid. I'm not blind. I saw you clearly but before I could talk, you slipped the bag to your friend."

The crowd started getting restless.

"All this talk won't help us. Let's kill the man," somebody from the crowd demanded. All around the crowd erupted, shouting "Yes! Yes!"

"Let's give him the benefit of the doubt. He might be talking the truth," said Somah as he tried to control the crowd.

"No! No! No! Let's kill him," the crowd chanted and again started slapping and kicking the suspect.

Suddenly, two ATU officers arrived on the scene. Brandishing their guns, they forced their way into the center of the crowd. The crowd dispersed as people fled in panic. The Anti Terrorist Unit was feared. Only the suspect, the victim, Somah, and a few onlookers who were watching the scene from a safe distance remained.

"What's the problem here?" the taller of the two soldiers, who later identified himself as Captain Duo, shouted.

"It's my bag, my handbag," the victim blabbed.

"Your bag? What about your bag?"

"He stole my handbag." She pointed at the suspect. "He jerked my handbag and gave it to his friend who ran away with it." The lady burst out crying again.

"He jerked your bag? Where's the bag, mister?" the second soldier asked.

"It's not true, officer. I have no bag. I jerked no bag from her. I'm innocent," the suspect pleaded.

"Why would she accuse you falsely? Sound and full-grown woman like this, she will just lie on you if you did nothing to her? Why didn't she accuse any other person but you?"

"That's my bad luck, sir," replied the suspect, looking a little bit relieved now.

"What does the bag contain?" asked Captain Duo, staring at the lady. "Money or material?"

"Both," the woman sobbed. "My cellphone and other people's money."

"How much is it?"

"Three hundred seventy-five US dollars, along with two thousand five hundred Liberian dollars!"

"How long has it been since your bag was stolen?" the captain asked again.

"About an hour now," she replied between sobs.

"I have risked talking for him, trying to make him return the woman's handbag, but he refused to admit that he stole it," Somah interjected.

The two ATU soldiers now glanced at each other, obviously not sure of how to tackle the problem. By then, the ring of onlookers and sympathizers started to swell again.

After a brief impasse, the soldiers decided to take the matter to their sub-base at Happy Corner, UN Drive. The crowd had to pass through the main avenue, Water Street, in order to reach their destination. As they were passing through, more people joined them. Even market women abandoned their wares to steal a glance.

As the crowd passed by the police depot, two policemen standing in front of the building were about to intercept and disperse the crowd. But when they saw the two ATU soldiers they retreated instantly.

"Why these soldiers keep usurping our functions? They always poke their noses into what is not their business," one of the policemen said to the other as they watched the crowd. "Their business is to stay at their barracks or keep on their bases. They have no right arresting people or handling civil matters."

"Look. You know that once these old rebels have tasted power, they can't do without it," the lieutenant replied. "Worst of all, they have come to town and their *pa-pay* Taylor is now president. They will look for any opportunity to gain attention and make some extra money."

They waited until the crowd walked by, and then the lieutenant continued, "In fact, I have the mind to go and stop them. They have no right...and we shouldn't sit by and allow this to continue."

"Ah! Stop them? You must be joking, comrade," his colleague said. "You want to go, unarmed as you are, and challenge those heartless guys with their automatic rifles? Without doubt, you have the mind and heart and even the guts to confront them, but remember, they will certainly grind you to dust. I wouldn't try it even if I was paid one million dollars."

Somah, eager to get home now, didn't follow the crowd. Instead he made straight for the bus parking, past the murmuring policemen. When he reached the parking, there were five minibuses, but only one was bound for Barnersville. That meant he had to fight his way through to get on. He finally got on and took his seat. Soon the bus door was shut and it rolled away slowly across the Old Bridge over the Mesurado River. It was like a chartered trip. There were no short stops along the way. On the bus there were talks, one after another, about the status quo in the nation. Somebody started the talk about the resurgence of war in Lofa.

"The war is getting serious and spreading gradually, just like how it started in Nimba," someone said. "People taking it for joke."

Another person began talk about the Christmas season. "This season will be much better, unlike last season. Almost every thing is being sold at half their normal prices or less."

A woman raised a salient point: the issue of brutality by state security, and the culture of impunity that was becoming ever so common.

But Somah's mind was far off. He barely heard anything. His mind was on the incident down Waterside. Would the woman ever get back her handbag and find everything intact? What would become of the alleged culprit if he failed to confess? Or would the ATU soldiers connive with him? Was he actually guilty?

Somah was jolted out of his thoughts when the bus made its first stop just after the Gardnersville Supermarket area, somewhere near Barnersville Junction. Good thing the bus did stop because those thoughts were beginning to overwhelm Somah's mind.

A fellow sitting behind Somah rose and descended the bus. He reached into his back pocket for his wallet to pay the carboy his fare, but his hand felt nothing. The wallet was gone. Someone had cunningly cut his jeans pocket, perhaps with a razor blade, and slipped off with the wallet.

"Oh, my God! I'm finished!" he screamed nervously, his hand passing through the pocket. "Someone has damaged me!"

Somah felt so sorry for the man. The wallet might contain all of his money. An air of suspicion hung about the place and it made Somah shiver.

"Eh, my people! Who has done this wickedness?" a woman sitting on the design-seat of the bus shouted, indignant.

"This might have happened down Waterside," another passenger said. "Those guys are as desperate as wounded lions now."

"I wouldn't doubt that," a fellow sitting by Somah nodded in agreement. "Bunch of rogues! They stand in line and pretend as if they were passengers too."

"You don't think it happened when you were getting on the bus?" the driver asked from behind his steering wheel.

"No. The wallet was still on me when I got on the bus," the man snapped, his voice shaky. "This thing happened on the bus."

Everyone looked at each other with puzzled expressions. In sympathy with the victim, the passengers on board the bus agreed to be searched for the missing wallet. One by one they descended and waited, after being thoroughly searched. Soon, the last one, a smartly-dressed, decent-looking guy, came rushing down from the bus.

"Here's your wallet," he said, handing it over to the man who had reported it missing. "I found it under the seat." He spoke quite shamelessly and without remorse. Then in haste he paid the carboy and, before anyone could shout "Rogue! Rogue!" he was far across the street, half running, half walking, barely escaping being run over by a speeding jeep, and soon slipped out of sight.

In the wallet, besides a few Liberian dollars, was $1,500 US dollars the man had just received from abroad via Western Union on behalf of family members. The man stood there shivering and almost speechless. He managed to express his gratitude to everyone for helping him get back his wallet and his money. Clinging to the wallet, the man hastened homeward, his heart probably pounding at his ribs.

Somah and his fellow passengers climbed back on the bus and the driver pulled away. As the rest of the passengers talked on and on about the incident, Somah looked out the window, sitting hunched and mute in his seat, staring on in disbelief.

M. Woryonwon Roberts

Back in the early 2000s, there was a special fea-
ture on BBC's *Network Africa* program called *True
Crime Stories*. The program hosted solicited entries
from listeners across Africa. Many contributed personal experiences, or firsthand accounts of crimes in their
respective towns and cities. I decided I would send
something from Liberia, too. I wrote a short piece, but
never submitted it. A few months later, the prevailing
state of affairs at the time—the hustle and bustle of
daily life so worthy to be captured in words—nudged
me to work on the piece again, and it became a short
story called *Between Crimes*. Life in Monrovia was so
constricted at the time I wrote. Society was charged
with lots of vexing social issues: fear, hatred and inse-

curity, violence, crime and impunity. People's rights were being violated daily. There was disappointment and frustration over the way things were being run in the country. All around I could see on people's faces anger and vengeance, and simple incidents flared up into shocking episodes of great proportion.

With this story, I wish to discourage the notion of subscribing to theft, or crimes, as a means of taking a short cut in life instead of working to earn a livelihood. In this vein, affirmative action—people's collective action so to speak—is a valuable asset. Although sometimes violent and sometimes peaceful (I'm in no way a fan of violence though), people's power is almost always effective in every society. When people are pressed or threatened by certain societal circumstances or ills, they feel compelled to decide and act together swiftly to solve the problem, or address the issue at hand. That power merits notice! I want this fact to resonate with readers.

Monrovia Rain
Augustus Y. Voahn

It has been going on for the whole day, non-stop. The city has darkened. The streets are wet and the market places are muddy and flooded. No one, big or small, seems to like it. Everyone and everything seems to be defenseless against it. It makes one mad, but there's nothing you can do about it. It's cold, extremely cold. And everyone feels it, whether you are walking, working, or eating. Even if you decide to jog to produce heat, it does no good. A short run from the side of the road into a waiting taxi makes one drenched to the bone, makes you sick. A sick day, a sick city. When will it ever stop? It doesn't want to stop. It comes down slowly but heavily. Every single drop is capable of sousing you up. It is Monrovia Rain. Slow rain, endless rain, heavy rain, and merciless rain.

As the rain came, it bathed the Joe Bar Market. Washed it, cleaned it, then muddied and flooded it, right along with the whole Old Road community. Poor marketeers with a leaking roof above their heads were defenseless against the impact, some clustering to one another for body warmth, others hiding under the table for shelter, still others protecting their goods with their bodies.

He was right in the middle of the mud, taking one step after another with difficulty. Stepping here, stepping there. The mud splashing all over him and in his eyes, on his head. Mud, rain, tears, dirt, wetness. He was in the open. No cover over his head, and every single dry space taken.

There he was in the rain, soaked, drenched and cold to the bone. He was laughing and crying too. Water dripping all over him, from his hair and rolling down. Tears rolling down the eyes, slimy liquid running down the nostrils. But why was he laughing? Because suffering has been his way of life. Laughing the only way to keep himself alive.

The people were laughing and clapping, shouting out names at him. All sorts of names. Fine names, ugly names, funny names, and dirty names. He responded in a very special way to every one of those names. Either with a dancing stroke, or a jump, or laughter. He was out there in the open with the heavy downpour showering him while they were all sheltered under different sorts of makeshift roofs. He was putting on a show for the people in the rain. They love him for the shows, for it always makes them laugh. He has three empty bottles in his hands—the remaining goods of the day. Business has not been good today. He started out early this morning with five empty bottles for sale. That's his business. That and his singing and dancing. His only means of earning a cent. And how does he eat? A ten-dollar bowl of bulgur wheat at the end of the day usually solves the problem for that day only. Then he retires to bed under the last tables in the corner, on the chilly cold market floor. With rats and roaches as sleeping companions, he sleeps soundly, has great dreams and wakes up early in the morning to start the hustle again.

He is very popular around here. Everyone knows him. He is a friend to them all –from bony fish sellers to red oil sellers, from bulgur wheat sellers to kokodolo sellers. They all like him. They like him for his friendliness, his jokes, his dirtiness and stinking smells. But most of all they like him for his songs. He sings for anything, a piece of fish, a piece of kola nut, a cup of kokodolo or bulgur wheat. He knows all the marketeers by name and everyone knows him by a name. He has more than a dozen, and everyone uses the one they like. From Joe Bloggs to Johnny Walker, Brown Beans to Bulgur Wheat, or Bubba John. But among all, one name has surfaced. He is known by all as Poor Joe. Poor Joe is the one name that everyone knows.

∼

Little Poor Joe is twelve years old. The story goes that he once had a father, a loving mother and some brothers and sisters. Poor Joe had a home. He used to sleep on a spongy mattress, and he ate three square meals a day. The story even continues that Poor Joe once went to school. It may be true because he says the alphabet from A to O, and the numbers from 1 to 15. But where are his dear father and mother? Where are his brothers and sisters? And what happened to the three square meals a day?

Well, the story also goes that a few years ago when Poor Joe was about seven years old, there was this big war with shooting, fighting, killing. Who was shooting who and for what, Poor Joe had no idea. Anyway he woke up one morning to the terrible sound of guns everywhere. Mama and Papa scared didn't know what to do, so they packed a few things and began to go. Going where, who knows? Then all of a sudden, a group of armed men appeared from nowhere. What are they going to do? Kill Mama and Papa? No it can't be. But oh! Look! Right there before Poor Joe's eyes Mama and Papa were shot and killed. Then his brothers and sisters. His swift feet saved him, and that's how Poor Joe is left without Mama and Papa, without a home and no more three square meals a day, the story concludes.

But that was a long time ago; two or three years or even five years now, six maybe, no one exactly remembers and no one cares. The story has lost its edge of pity. After all there are so many Poor Joes in the city. So what? As long as he is here to sing and dance and make people laugh, no problem.

Poor Joe has known no home besides Joe Bar Market. He's been around since…no one remembers when. But he's here every day, rain or shine. Everyone in this market is his mother, father, brother and sister.

Today, it is raining. It is really pouring down and Poor Joe is in the rain. There he is at the far end of the market in the open area, the fire coal section. He's in the black dirty and stinking mud stepping here and there with bottles in his hands. The people are laughing, cheering at him. But what is he actually doing in the rain? Making some kind of rain show? Well guess not, Poor Joe is just finding his way through the mud. Just because he's Poor Joe, everything he does is poor and funny. When he is eating people laugh, when he talks people laugh, when he sings and dances, people laugh till tears come down.

Well that's Poor Joe again and he's dancing in the rain this time. All of a sudden a tall fellow with a bushy beard approaches from nowhere. Strange thing. Is he going to jump in the rain just to talk to a guy like Poor Joe? And who is he anyway? The laughing and clapping have stopped, because Poor Joe himself has stopped and is looking up to see the stranger's face. Everyone is now concerned and looking.

"Small boy, what is your name?" the man asks.

"Hmm? What you say?" asks Poor Joe.

"I said what's your name?"

No one has ever been this concerned about Poor Joe before. To walk in the rain just to ask for his name? Besides, doesn't everybody know his name around here anyway?

"My name Poor Joe," he manages to reply.

"And what are you doing here, in the rain?"

"Well I dancing, I walking, I selling my bottles."

"Then why are the people laughing at you?"

"Because they like my dancing."

"So what will they give you?" the man asks.

"Sometimes they give me one leaflet or two," says Poor Joe.

"What is a leaflet?"

"Oh! You don't know leaflet!" he exclaims. "I mean David Vinton or Dutch or notes."

"Ooh! You mean money?"

"Yeah, Pa-pay."

"Where is your house?" asks the man.

"Here," answers Poor Joe boldly.

"Where?"

"I stay right here in this market! What happened na?!"

"Where are your people?"

"I na get nobody."

"Ooh! I see," says the stranger. "Do you know the Regular Boys Home?"

"What dey call Boysoom?" asks Poor Joe.

By this time the crowd has become disinterested in what is going on, and begins dispersing. Poor Joe does not understand what this inquiry is leading to. He thinks about running from the stranger, but something inside of him tells him to hold on. There is something unusual about this acquaintance.

"Poor Joe, I want to tell you something," the man continues. If you agree to what I'm going to tell you, things will be all right. Take that straight road and go to the Catholic Hospital junction. Look on your left, you will see a big white fence. Enter it and ask for one man called Father Dee. He will help you.

Even though he does not understand what this man is getting at, Poor Joe does not ask any questions. There is something divine about this acquaintance. A strange kind of feeling overwhelms him, and keeps him complying with the man.

~

It takes Poor Joe about twenty minutes to find the Regular Boys Home. He goes to the gate wet and dripping with water all over. The little T-shirt on him now clings to his skin.

"Who you come to, pekin?" the security guard at the gate asks.

"I came to Father Boys Home," replied Poor Joe.

The security guard laughs. "Father Boys Home! Who sent you?"

"Da one man say I muh come to him so he can help me," answers Poor Joe.

"This is the Regular Boys Home, and you mean Father Dee. Come let's go to him." Poor Joe is led by the hand to see Fr. Dee.

Fr. Dee is a jolly, jovial Missionary. He came to Liberia sometime ago to accomplish the dream of one great man called Don Bosco: to transform wolves into sheep, and to take care of guys like Poor Joe. The ever-smiling priest is in a big circle in an open field behind the big building. He is surrounded by at least seventy-five boys of the same age as Poor Joe. They are just relaxing, conversing, joking and laughing hilariously like buddies.

From around the corner, Poor Joe appears, accompanied by the security guard. His appearance draws attention. All the boys stop their laughing and all eyes turn on him. One person is soon to be added to their number and they know it well. As for Poor Joe he is yet to understand what this is all about. He is kind of confused. He still does not understand why he was led to this man, or why all those boys are around him so. Anyway, Poor Joe finally appears before Fr. Dee.

"This boy came to see you, Father," says the security guard.

"You are welcome, my boy," says Fr. Dee. Poor Joe hardly knows what to answer in return.

"What is your name?" asks Fr. Dee.

"I na get one name, I get plenty name."

"Oh, which one should we call you?"

"Call me Brown Beans or call me Bulgur Wheat. No, wait! Let's see...call me Kokodolo. No, Poor Joe. Yes, call me Poor Joe. Da my real name."

"Poor Joe! What a name!" exclaims Fr. Dee. "So Poor Joe, what can I do for you?"

"What you say?"

"I say what you come here for?"

"They say I muh come here."

"They say, who say?"

"One man who met me to the Joe Bar Market."

"So what kind of help do you want?" asks Fr. Dee.

"I want some kokodolo," answers Poor Joe.

"But first, do you have a place to live?"

"Yes."

"Where?"

"In the market."

"I mean where are your parents? Your father and mother?"

"I na get father and mother."

"What happened to them?"

"Da de war."

"Would you like to live here?"

Poor Joe carefully turns around and takes a long and thoughtful look at the boys all sitting around peacefully in a circle. They all look happy, clean, and healthy, and their eyes seem to be telling him "stay, and be one of us." He sees a big difference between the boys and himself. Why are the boys different from him? Can he be like them? All of a sudden Poor Joe is overwhelmed by a deep yearning inside of him to be like those boys. There is a new look on his face. He cannot comprehend it, but it is happening. He really wants to stay and become one of those boys.

He can now see the difference between him and the boys. He can imagine what they have that he lacks. They have almost everything he doesn't have. They have food, shelter, clothing. And in abundance, too! This is the first time that Poor Joe has ever dreaded his life out there in the cold and the rain. Without knowing it he hears himself shouting out loud, "Father, Father! Please let me stay, I don't want to go anywhere again. I want to live here, I want to live with you, I want to be like them," pointing towards the rest of the boys tearfully.

"Okay, okay. We want you to stay." Turning towards the rest of the boys, Fr. Dee asks:
"Do you want our new friend to stay?"
"Yeaaa!" they chorus.
"So let's say welcome to our new friend!"
"Welcome!"
"Welcome!"

"Fine," says Fr. Dee. "Everyone is happy to have you join us. You will have a place to sleep and enough food to eat. Be happy, make friends and join in and play the games you see them playing. Can you play football?"
"No," answers Poor Joe.

"Can you jump?"

"No."

"So what can you do?"

"I can sing and dance."

"Oh great! So we have a new music man here! Would you like us to hear one of your songs?"

"Yes," says Poor Joe with a smile. Then he thinks about his old song. That song. That emotional song. The one he always uses to draw money out of rich people's pockets. It's a lyric that he composed himself to explain his plight to people. When Poor Joe sings this song, no one can be so callous as to keep their tears from flowing down. Even though he hardly ever pities his own condition, this lyric sometimes makes Poor Joe cry himself.

He positions himself, and takes his usual stance: left hand resting on the heart right hand stretched forward. He looks into the eyes of the boys around him, as if seeking their approval before starting. They are all watching, giggling with delight, anxious to see this new show. When he receives their approval, with a dozen smiles, he begins.

Where place my mama eh?
Where place my mama eh?
Ziki twinkle, ziki twinkle

Where place my papa eh?
Where place my papa eh?
Ziki twinkle, ziki twinkle.

They kill my mama o!
They kill my mama o!
I can't see her again.

They kill my papa o!
They kill my papa o!
I can't see him again.

The words, sorrow and emotions engulf the whole gathering like a spell. Everyone becomes completely silent. As he sings, some of the boys thinking about their own situation begin to weep. This song seems to tell their stories. What had happened to Poor Joe in this song happened to almost all of them. He is singing, not just his own song, but also their song. Poor Joe is their mouthpiece, pleading with the world to come to their aid. Yes, they see themselves in him.

Fr. Dee stands there transfixed, not knowing what to say after the music has died down. Tears begin dripping from his eyes. The song explains it all, he thinks to himself. This little boy needs me. He needs my help, and all that I can offer. He needs a guide to direct him in the right direction, to recognize his talents and improve them. It is my responsibility and I need people to join me in this process, for as the Lord said, the harvest is plentiful, but the laborers are few.

For a few seconds Fr. Dee stands there thinking to himself. Then he orders some of his boys: "Take him in, show him where to take a bath, and find some new

clothes for him. Then give him sufficient food to eat."
To the others he says, "Go prepare another bed and
mattress, and put a new sheet on it for him."

Poor Joe is taken by the hand, and led by some
boys his age. For the first time in years he has a real
satisfactory bath – a hot soapy bath. He's given new
clothes, new jean trousers, a T-shirt and sneakers. He
looks glamorous in them. In the dining room, he sits
in a chair, at a brown wooden table, and is served. For
the first time in years he has a decent meal to eat. Oh!
How delicious the food is! It has a special taste, a taste
he has not had in many years. As he eats, he can think
of no one but his mother. Yes, she used to cook just
like this. He clearly remembers. Right there before
his eyes, he can see her in the kitchen, dishing out,
putting it in his special bowl that Papa bought from
Waterside Market. "Mama, I am back from school…
where is my food?" he would ask. "Just look in the
cupboard sonny," she would say.

When night comes, Poor Joe is shown his bed. A
little bed with a spongy mattress, in the middle of the
room, surrounded by other ones just like it. He cannot believe his eyes. A bed, a bed! When did he last
sleep in a bed? So many years ago, he can't remember.

That night he makes a lot of friends, who are
so kind to him. Among them are Archie, Tamba,
Emmanuel, Prince and Momo. There was only one
who was not very friendly. "I am Baboon the Beautiful," the boy said, with his long mouth. "Ask everyone

about me. When you try me I'll show you this place with one punch in the face." Baboon was immediately calmed down by Archie and Emmanuel, who threatened to deal with him if he continued.

For the first time in months, Poor Joe slept really soundly and peacefully, with wonderful dreams.

A sweet night is always short. The sun is up, bright and early. There are long shining rays penetrating their way through the holes in the window and waking him up from his sleep. Bright and powerful beams shooting straight into his eyes. Poor Joe blinks. For a minute he doesn't know where he is. Oh! Of course, this is Joe Bar Market, ground floor. But who's this crazy guy pointing a torch light into my face? Wait a minute! This isn't Joe Bar Market! Oh! Wait! I'm lying on a bed, and it's sunlight. "The sun!" Poor Joe is shouting at the top of his voice now. He jumps from the bed, dashes towards the door, flies straight through it and out onto the porch. He remembers everything now.

Out on the porch, Poor Joe looks into the sky. It is white and cloudless. Old daddy sun is smiling sweetly on nature and on him. There is no more rain in the air. Oh! The sun, the sun, it is shining everywhere and on everything in the city. Yes, the sun is shining on Poor Joe now. The wetness, damp, mud, slime, yes, the rain... all is drying away. The city is getting dry again. Life is returning to the city and to him. Yes, the sun, it shines. It's shining now and bringing life, joy and happiness too. The sun is here, drying away those wet and rainy nights. Yes, the sun has finally come. It is here at long last. Those dark and rainy days are gone, gone and never to return. The sun is here now. It has come. Life has come. Real life. New life. It's like being born again. The sun, at long last.

Augustus Y. Voahn

Monrovia Rain was written in 1994. That was a time of war, hunger, unemployment and homelessness in Monrovia, and I was working as a young social worker with Don Bosco Homes. DBH was a religious institution for homeless children. As field workers our job was to reach out to homeless street children—mainly boys—and offer them a shelter where they could be fed, protected, and perhaps reunified with family. My role was to interview each kid and write down his story. After a while, my head was flooded with hundreds of different stories. I was a walking documentarian or biographer. It was through the documentation of

50

these many stories that I got the inspiration to write *Monrovia Rain*. Another major inspirational factor was the rains that fall in Monrovia. Rainy Season in Monrovia is merciless. When the rains come they soak the city through and through. One evening on my way home from work, the rains suddenly came down and soaked me through. All the work documents I had with me got spoiled that evening. I was so angry with the rain that I didn't know what to do. I reached home and found hot water to take a bath. Then I began feeling better. It was at that point that it came dawning on me....I said to myself, *If one like me who has a house to sleep in can feel the terrible impact of this rain, then what about the homeless boys sleeping out there in the open? Do I know what will happen to them under this heavy downpour?* I had no answer. That night I tossed and turned, traumatized by the rain and thoughts of the street children. A few weeks later I started writing *Monrovia Rain*. The story just flowed freely through my head to the pen, and Poor Joe found himself drenched like I was.

Unfortunately, boys like Poor Joe find themselves on the wrong side of society. I mean if you compare them with other children in stable homes with parents, you see a big gap and you can't but feel pity. We must understand that street children are not responsible for their conditions. They have no choice. The society places them in that slot, and back in 1994 we could also blame the war for their condition. The politicians who determine the direction of the country usually do not even consider guys like Poor Joe in making their decisions. A better social welfare program is required to change things, but the problem is that the government usually does not prioritize such desperately needed interventions. They always leave it with NGOs to do their work for them. Unfortunately, NGOs do not intervene holistically in the entire country's problems. They only target a small portion of the country and support a few people while the majority continues to suffer. Wealthy individuals in our society need to be more involved in coming to the aid of the many Poor Joes around us too. Organizations and people who come to the rescue of marginalized populations are to be recognized by the authorities and commended. They have to be encouraged by being rendered more cooperation from the government. They have to be facilitated in many ways and protected from huge taxation and harsh regulations. The government needs to be more proactive and serious about the social welfare of the disadvantaged population of Liberia—not only street boys, but the physically, visually and mentally challenged population of our country as well.

The problem of street children and homelessness still exists in our society today, but perhaps not to the same degree as it was when I wrote *Monrovia Rain*. The situation has also taken many different dimensions. Currently in Liberia there are many fatherless and motherless children living with aunts and uncles who simply use them to do street selling and other chores. The education of these children is never prioritized. They are used to bring income to other people. Some of the girls are even used for prostitution and trafficked across borders. Our children in general remain vulnerable in a careless society, and we need to do more in terms of their protection.

Another Dead Girl
Gii-Hne S. Russell

The girl sat at the table in a bar, sipping occasionally from a glass of Coca Cola. There were also bottles
of Fanta and Sprite on the table. There could have
been Club Beer, Stout and even Heineken and whis-
key if the bar was a big time one, but it wasn't. It was
one of those hastily erected structures made of mats
and a relief-issued plastic covering which someone
had put together for the Christmas and New Year season, but had not yet taken down or at least improved.

The girl regretted somewhat having accepted too
many soft drinks, and fought the temptation to give
the drinks back and ask for the money. But why worry? It, in fact, was a shameful thought. She would
gulp those two extra bottles down or share them with

somebody. No, not with anybody. It was better to gulp them down. This was her first time being offered three bottles of soft drinks and she had to enjoy herself.

It was almost noon, and the bar had only a few customers. The owner of the place was relaxing in a squeaky rattan chair while her workers prepared for the evening rush hour. Another woman kept eyeing the girl quizzically. It was as if she wanted to talk to the girl but couldn't bring herself to do so.

The girl finished the Coca Cola and relaxed. She had to let it 'go down' before drinking either the Fanta or Sprite. In the meantime, she pondered over the fortune that had befallen her. She could still scarcely believe that it was real. It was like a dream too grand to be true! All her problems were over now. There would be no more want for clothing or money. There would be no more stabbing pains of hunger which pride could suppress outwardly but not inwardly. No more going up and down 'looking for it' when it could not be found because she could neither afford the price for it nor the face to beg for it. She would be in school again, a good school too. Maybe William Booth, Calvary Temple, or the Rock High School. Or she would go to any of those big schools in Monrovia with uniforms that had all eyes on you. But whatever, she would be in school.

Another thing this fortune offered was that she wouldn't be pestered by anyone anymore. The good for nothing boys, the irresponsible men, and the lions-dressed-as-lambs who shamelessly compete in ruining the lives of young girls and even children, would stay away from her. She would say to them with pride: "I have a lover." Her friends who called her stupid for refusing men whom they said were ready to spend money on a girl just to be able to call her name, would respect her when she showed Mackie to them. They would finally agree with her that a girl doesn't have to advertise or sell her body to men for money in order to live.

Oh handsome, good Mackie! She praised God in her heart for sending Mackie to her. He was tall and light in complexion. His hair, which was always treated with one of those rich hair products, was shining black and wavy. She had seen Mackie once or twice around the community a long time ago. But it was only in the last month that he began crossing her path frequently. Then a week ago they met and became friends. There was something unusual about him that got her attracted to him on that first encounter, but she had effectively guarded herself against such things as physical appearance and holdings. She didn't flee from him as she would have normally done, but she kept her distance.

Then three days ago he told her. He told her he loved her so much that he was ready to give his life to her. He was for her, only her. He told her about himself, how he was not like other boys and how he wanted a girl who would love him and not break his heart. What he told her was not just the 'sweet talk' other boys and men were known for. She hardly had time for sweet talk because she knew it was bait that men and boys used to lure girls to their beds. But Mackie was sincere so she listened and didn't flee. To be honest, perhaps it was also because she had never been in the tight corner she was in. The friends who she stayed with were getting intolerant of her 'acting like Holy Mary' on them. They were saying that because she would never sell her body, it was a liability to them who were selling their bodies.

Not far from the bar was the motel where Mackie had taken her that morning. It was a surprise when he told her why they were there, but for some reason, she didn't refuse this time. A tinge of pain flashed through her mind when she remembered what they did there, how he did her and left her sore. It was not the way she had anticipated knowing a man. She felt stained. But it was all right now. Mackie loved her. In fact he even loved her more now. He was a good boy. With the corner she was in getting tighter and tighter, he would be her rescuer. It was all right now. Mackie was from a rich family, even though he downplayed their wealth. His mother was constantly asking to see his girlfriend, he said, and his whole family would be happy to see her. Yes, it was all right now. He would soon be back to take her to his family.

The girl opened the Fanta and poured it into the glass. Soon the Fanta was finished and the Sprite followed. When she looked at the clock, it was going to two. Mackie should have been back by now. He said he was going to get his laptop from a friend. Maybe the friend was not home and he was waiting. I just have to wait, she thought.

2:15, and still no Mackie.

The woman who had been watching her now got up and started to walk towards her. Maybe because I am using up the space, the girl thought, even though there were many vacant tables.

"Hello, my daughter," the woman said.
"Hello Ma."
"Your name?"
"Atina."
"You're waiting for somebody?"
"Yeah."
"The tall, bright boy who you came with?"
"Yes."
"Who is he to you?"
The girl weighed the question in her mind. Who was Mackie really to her? Her boyfriend? They had just met and didn't know each other well. Or were they just friends? It had to be a boyfriend. Not quite yet, but that was it. He said he loved her, after all.

"He's my boyfriend," she replied. "He told me to wait here and went to get his computer. He'll soon be back and then we will leave."

The woman sighed and gave her the look a mother would give a child who never follows advice and keeps falling in one trouble after another. Then the questions came. Was she in school? No, she dropped out in the 10th grade due to the lack of money. Where did she live? She lived in Seventy-second with some friends because she ran away from the home of the woman she had lived with since before she knew herself. Why did she flee from that woman in the first place? She fled due to tension in the family. The foster father had her in his mind and the woman thought she was after her man. How old was she? She was almost 17.

The woman then told the girl what she knew about the handsome, good, loving and rich Mackie. In fact, his name was not even Mackie. That was just the first thing.

Atina walked back home slowly.

At first, Atina had doubted what the woman was saying about Mackie. So the woman had said "Call me dog if the so-called Mackie comes back." Atina had waited a whole hour more, and the lover boy didn't show face. She tried to sneak out but met the woman at the door. She murmured that she was leaving and the woman had looked at her sorrowfully and promised that the lover boy would never again be welcome at the bar. But that was not important to her.

Why was she so bad lucky? Why was God not helping her even though she tried to do the right thing? Were her friends right that all the good men and boys were in heaven and so the only thing a girl could do was to try, if possible, to get free money from the ones on earth or make them pay for every use of her body? Atina could not answer these questions. Bereft with hopelessness, broken hearted and angry, she was on a thin line between remaining with her friends to be a prostitute, or moving out, to where she didn't know. Her dreams, all her dreams, were lost now.

With her spirit so low, she felt dying would have been better. Pride told her to maintain an even face, but Broken Heart told tears to flow. Pride held till she left the main street, and then Broken Heart took over and tears spouted. She held the 150 Liberian Dollars Mackie gave her. It was but a smidgen to the school fees, the clothes, and everything she had anticipated. And to think that her virginity that she had piously kept was lost for only 150 LD and three soft drinks burst her heart more. Crying bitterly, her fingers gave way and the money slid from her palm.

Gii-Hne S. Russell

Another Dead Girl comes from an incident in my neighborhood concerning a girl and a young man. This guy tried to impress the girl he had newly met with wealth he didn't have. He told her that he was a big business man, and while he was 'bursting the girl's head,' as we say, some friends who were part of the scheme came asking about his cars, about his business, and about his houses.

I'm always looking for something to write about, and that incident with the 'bluff boy' had me thinking about the issue of how girls fall victim to men who use money and material things to lure them to bed. I don't know whether that girl fell for all those glib words, but I felt sorry for her and other gullible girls and young women who become victims in that way. Most of the time the affection and care dies after the men, as they say, 'know about' these girls.

Some girls are on the street because they want good things like phones, fine clothes, and shoes. They go after boys and men who can offer these things in exchange for sexual favors. Other girls are forced onto the street by their own parents and guardians who can't afford to take care of them or send them to school. The parents make the excuse that they're big enough to fend for themselves. You hear remarks like, 'A big girl like you can't buy soap for yourself?' or 'Fine girl like you don't have fitting clothes to wear?' These girls usually end becoming pregnant or becoming prostitutes. Some who get pregnant even end up dying from unsafe abortions.

In the years since I wrote the story, sexual exploitation has become even more rampant, and so has sexual looseness on the part of young people. Strong parental guidance is now considered old-fashioned, and boys and girls who submit to such guidance are called all sorts of names. Young children who are sent out to sell food and wares are exposed to all sorts of vices, and the so-called 'big shots' are chasing underage girls more than before.

The main message I want to show in *Another Dead Girl* is that not all girls 'on the street' are there because they are bad. We judge many of these girls and young women wrongly and as a result they are stuck in the lives they find themselves in because no one wants to help them get out. Many of them are forced be where they are. The fact is that many girls and boys are on the streets because they never had good and strong parents, or proper guidance. Yes, teenagers are prone to mistakes, but where there are good parents they will be able to recover from the consequences of their mistakes.

Homecoming
Vamba Sherif

I had been away for 20 years. I had spent most of that time in Belgium, a period during which Liberia was embroiled in civil war. What was bringing me home was the death of my mother and the contradictory accounts regarding the circumstances of her death. I had arrived in Monrovia from Brussels two days before, apprehensive about the journey because of the stories of people like me who had undertaken such trips and had died of poisons mixed into their food. After the civil war, poison had replaced bullets, I had been told, and the enemy was omnipresent.

I lodged at my elder brother Edmond's, in Gardnersville, a suburb of the city, where homes stood on marshlands, and where, when it rained, the water rose and burst what remained of the sewerage. My brother had taken several dozen family members into his care, mostly youngsters whose parents had not survived the war. He was a replica of my father, at least of that single memory of my father that I had held onto for more than 30 years. The memory was of a closely shaved man with a permanent frown around his brows, a man with a polished forehead that promised infinite youth. He was a businessman, and had owned a store located on the busiest street in Wologizi, the town of my birth. I remember him sitting in an arm-chair, drumming with his fingers while I, a four-year-old, played on the floor of his bedroom in our house. He had passed on a year later, leaving behind a void that I would struggle to fill, and now he was staring at me from the face of my brother. Edmond must now have been around the same age as our father when I was born, the same height, the same temperament, his occasional outbursts of anger laced with the affecting humor for which my father was famous.

The evening before my departure to Wologizi, I sat with my brother in the living room of his home, where one of the children in his care had prepared our food. It consisted of parboiled rice served with cassava leaves and smoked fish prepared with palm oil. While we ate he told me about the war. Like our father, Edmond once had a thriving store with goods purchased from Dubai and China, right in the heart of Monrovia, on Ashmun Street. But it had been destroyed in the war. Now he had partnered with one of our cousins and had opened up a small store, where he sold office wares on Camp Johnson Road.

Edmond had lived most of his life in Monrovia, and the stories that reached me in Wologizi during my childhood were of a fiercely ambitious man: he had opened up his first store while in secondary school, had expanded into a larger store and was about to open up a chain of stores, thereby doing what our family had been doing for ages, trading, when the war broke out. He had been married once, he told me, but his wife had left him during the war.

"At one point, she ran about Monrovia with a gun in hand with the purpose of killing me," he told me. "I don't know what I did to deserve such a fate. It was not an easy time then, but we survived."

As I listened to him, I had the feeling that he needed me, needed an audience to hear his story, as if in doing so he would relieve himself of the burden it had become. The longing to tell stories about the war, which I found in my brother that night, would manifest itself in many other people. Liberians longed to tell stories of war, even the most horrific ones.

"Never ask people about the absent ones," Edmond said, "for you might be shocked to learn that a childhood friend or a dear aunt or uncle had been killed, or worse, had joined the rebels in killing their own people. Just keep quiet and wait until you are told about the missing or the dead."

It worried me that I would have to wait to be told about the war, but he meant to protect me from those horrific accounts. What he did not know was that his advice would not shield me from being broken by the accounts of my mother's death.

Later, after we had had our meal, he asked me about Belgium. "Vali, we heard that you build cars in that country, and that your company has come to appreciate your talent so much that they've done everything to keep you from leaving them, even to visit us. Is that true? If so, then you've made us all proud."

It was not true. I was a mere factory worker in an industrial city in Belgium, and all I did was assemble truck parts for days on end, year in, year out. But I couldn't tell him that. He wouldn't have believed me. My story, which began with me as a factory worker who worked in shifts, six or seven days a week, had elevated me to the level of a designer of trucks.

I told my brother about my early years as a refugee, about my life in a refugee camp which housed people with similar stories of war and persecution. At the camp I had as a teacher an old professor from Bosnia, and as friends a family from Ethiopia, a Ghanaian who taught me to ride a bicycle, and a Nigerian who was so smart that he succeeded in saving money in a place where all thought that was impossible. As a refugee, my life was monotonous: I would have the same breakfast every morning, bread served with cheese or jam – then stamp my card daily to prove I was present, while waiting for a decision that was certain to change my life: the decision whether I could stay or must leave the country. To fill in the hours, I managed to befriend the man who went to the city every day to rent several films for the entertainment of the refugees. Because of my love of film, I was the one who chose what we would see. In the world of films, with their realities detached from the one at the camp, I felt at home. I would marvel at the freedom enjoyed by the volunteer workers who cooked and kept order at the camp, returning to their homes at the end of each day.

The constant news of the civil war in Liberia, which filled the papers and crowded the headlines, made me desperate to attempt to escape the cage of camp life. I learned to speak and write Flemish, and, by the time I was granted asylum, I was ready to work in the truck factory and to send most of my earnings home to those family members who had fled the war to Sierra Leone and Guinea.

"I worked seven days a week for years, trying to help the family," I told my brother.

He nodded. "Yes, you did," he said.

The war had broken him. He had had a stroke that had almost paralyzed him. Like the fighter that he was, he had done everything to be able to walk again, refusing to use a walking stick even during those moments when he needed it most. "Once I become attached to a walking stick, I will never get rid of it," he explained. "I'm still fighting the effect of the stroke. One of which is that I tend to forget things."

In dark corners of the living room, on the floor and on mats, my nephews and nieces sat, listening to us. Some were born during the war, and those who were born just before the war now had children of their own. Children had become parents who could not support their offspring, and all were dependent on my brother.

All around us, the night was restless: church songs, drums and rattles rent the air. Monrovia had turned into a noisy marketplace of God-seekers.

"The war has made people turn to the only thing that gives them some modicum of solace, and that is religion," Edmond said.

The heat was unbearable. My shirt clung to my body from sweat. And despite the care my brother had taken, spraying the bedroom and draping a huge net over the mattress that I shared with him, the mosquitoes managed to find their way to me. I hardly slept a wink. My lack of sleep, I realized, had less to do with the mosquitoes than with the death of my mother. When I attempted to inquire about the circumstances of her death, Edmond said: "It happened a long time ago. Let it be and try to be at peace with her death."

But I couldn't.

The driver came to pick me up at dawn. As protection against unforeseen circumstances, I decided to take some of my cousins with me as guards. We loaded the jeep with bags of rice and other foodstuffs for the family in Wologizi. By the time the city awoke, we were far beyond its borders. The driver was good. I marveled at how he skillfully avoided the potholes that littered the roads and, when I commented on this, he said without hesitation or shame, "I was a driver for a rebel faction during the war." He was sturdy like a wrestler, bowlegged and with bloodshot eyes, and he wore a cap and winter boots in a heat that had denied me sleep. The revelation numbed me; I was sitting beside a man who had actually participated in the war, who had probably killed.

My driver pulled over at a roadside restaurant in a town that was swathed in dust, where the asphalt petered out into dusty roads. We had been driving for hours.

"Just imagine, Chief," he told me, as we stuffed ourselves with rice served with a sauce of brown beans and smoked fish cooked with palm oil – the famous Liberian dish, *torbogee*. I was uncomfortable with the 'chief' title, for he was employing it either to mock me or to emphasize our difference, putting me on an unwanted pedestal. "I would be speeding at 120 miles per hour in a jeep without a windshield, my head just below the steering wheel, for fear a sniper might snatch it off. At the back of the jeep would be a fighter with a machine gun, letting his anger loose on everything that crossed our path. The mission would be to drive right into the heart of enemy territory, and fire a few RPGs before returning to the base."

As I listened to him, it struck me that he must have been in his teens when he went on those attacks. The war in which he had participated began in 1989 with a rebel group, led by Charles Taylor, aimed to oust the then president Samuel Doe, who had come to power in a bloody coup in 1980. But the Liberian conflict began much earlier, during the founding of the country, when free blacks and former slaves from America returned to Africa in 1822 to found a new republic based on liberty. These founders were at odds with indigenous groups who thrived along the coast of Liberia and in the interior. The inability to create a balanced society without discrimination ultimately led to the coup in 1980 and then to the civil war in 1989.

"We won the war, Chief," he told me.

But at what cost, I wondered, thinking of my mother. She had died when the north was cordoned off from the rest of Liberia by the rebel group to which my driver belonged, as they fought other groups for control over that territory. I was told that she had taken ill and died for lack of medicine, but a week later someone claimed to have seen her in a refugee camp in Guinea. I even had a telephone call from a cousin in Guinea saying that my mother wanted to speak with me. But the information proved baseless. My mother had indeed passed on and I was left with questions as to how she had actually died. In subsequent years, I had attempted to visit her grave but had been hampered by reports of war, by lack of adequate funds or by the terrible condition of the roads which made it impossible to travel during rainy seasons.

Once we took to the road again, dust settled with solemnity in the car, impeding breath and sometimes blinding us. Flanking the road toward the north were forests, dense, perpetual and mysterious, the greenest of the green, crowning mountains and spreading like a canopy over the earth. Along the road, people traded coal, vegetables or bushmeat, or waited to be given a lift. Towns and villages emerged before us, some abandoned, others sparsely inhabited, but always with beautiful flame trees, which my eyes would caress, as if I were seeing them for the first time. This overwhelming beauty was a stark contrast to the country's recent history.

We arrived at Wologizi just before dusk. Its suburbs were cluttered with houses so dilapidated that I could not imagine human beings inhabiting them. One of the buildings I recognized at the heart of the city was a two-story building that once belonged to a Lebanese nicknamed 'Old Baldhead'. The people of Wologizi were ingenious at giving nicknames. The best local footballer was called 'The Broom' because he swept up everything in his path with his bare feet – player, ball and all. And the child who once torched a box in which his friend was hiding in an attempt to lure him out was named 'Foday, The Torturer,' which stuck so well that when I met him 20 years later, now old and wise and with a career in the agricultural sector, he was still called 'The Torturer,' but always behind his back. We had a corpulent man as teacher who, because of his size, the town named after a mountain. This teacher was versed in Shakespeare and would quote lines from Othello and Hamlet as if he were from a bygone era. But his jokes were often so spicy with sexual innuendos that women fled on seeing him. Rumor had it that he slept with most of them.

The Lebanese's building was bullet-ridden, bare of paint and dark with mold, like most homes around it. The main thoroughfare, where girls fried fish and *kala* at night to sell to lovers, appeared much narrower than I recalled, and the shops that once flanked it, including the gas station where checkers players often gathered to insult each other, were gone.

On that road in my early teens, when I was not swimming in the nearby river, or joining friends to play out in the moonlight, I would be singing songs from Indian films, or playing the heroes or the villains of those films – so much so that those who could not afford the entrance fee would give me some coins so that I could play out the films to them, including the songs. I was so adept at this that, whenever I played the villain Amjad Khan in an Amitabh Bachchan film, my audience would scatter in fright before me. I dreamed of becoming an actor, the African Bachchan, and of going to India and taking Bollywood by storm.

My heart skipped a beat as we turned the corner and drove into a road towards home. On my right was a school building that belonged to one of my uncles, a businessman who started out fetching firewood and selling it, later becoming one of the richest men in Wologizi. We drove past the school and slowly edged our way toward the compound which had once sizzled with life. During my childhood, on any given day, there would be more than 200 people in our compound, and the drama that played out within the shaded rooms and corners had shaped my outlook on life. I stepped out of the jeep and walked toward the compound. The family was standing in a small group, consisting mostly of women and children, the remnants of what had once been the largest family in Wologizi. As the women hugged me, I could smell firewood on them, the dust of pounded rice, and the food they were preparing. I held them tight, reluctant to let go, those women of my brothers and uncles who had been killed or had died during the war.

Afterwards, I paused to take in the compound. Some of the houses, including my mother's, were gone; so were the plum and butterpear trees I had often climbed to pick their fruits. But my father's house was still standing. I entered it now in search of the room I used to share with my siblings; the room in which, when I found myself alone, I would rehearse my role in films, striving to perfect the art of impersonations, the art of speaking Hindi or Bengali or Mandarin. I would be so swept away by those roles that, whenever I emerged from them, the world looked quite unreal to me. One day, I convinced my mother to accompany me to a film in which Amitabh Bachchan, who played its hero, was killed. My mother left the cinema in tears. "They murdered that handsome man," she said. "Why did they murder that good man?" That was the beginning and the end of her movie adventure. But every day after school I would assist the owner of the cinema, a man with a jaundiced face who had a lilt to his steps, by running errands for him or doing chores around his house in exchange for seeing a film. The movies were invariably Indian or Chinese, some of which I saw a dozen times. The passion for film never left me. But then the war broke out in Liberia, and I had to redream my life.

On coming out of the room, I met my brother Sekou waiting for me in what was once our father's room, the largest room in the house, and was now occupied by several women. It had lost some of its former grandeur: the chair in which my father often sat, drumming his fingers on its wooden arms, was gone, as was his smell. Every trace of him had been obliterated. The walls seemed new, the fresh painting had erased the old. There are many ways of erasing the past without much effort on one's part. The attempt to keep the house standing had replaced the importance of holding onto its history: my father's presence.

"Tell me what happened to our mother," I said to my brother.

He hesitated. "What do you mean?" he asked.

"I want to know how she died," I said.

"It was at the height of war. She was in Koniyan and fell ill. She died for lack of medicine," he said, avoiding my gaze.

Of all my brothers, Sekou was the one closest to me in looks and temperament. He understood my deepest fears, even with the distance that separated us, and when we communicated he would often surprise me with his insights. "You always say that you will return home," he once told me. "But what is home? You've been away for so long that I don't think this is your home any more."

Now he turned to me. "What do you want me to tell you?" he asked.

I did not answer.

My mother was the daughter of a scholar to whom miracles were attributed. It was said that no one had taught him, and he was famous for lecturing the whole night without consulting a book. Everything he owned, he shared with his brothers, and was generous to a fault. The man, after whom I was named, had risen to such a stature, that the presidents of Liberia and Sierra Leone sought his advice and prayers. He always preached peace and insisted that a religion that divided brothers and sisters and made one feel superior to the other was no religion at all but a divisive doctrine. It won him many admirers but made him controversial. When he passed on in Gbarnga, a place where there was no mosque and where he was but a guest, the people of the city who did not adhere to his faith but who regarded him nevertheless as one of their own insisted that he be buried by them. The President of Liberia had to intervene, especially when the Muslims insisted that he belonged to them. The President ruled that the people of Gbarnga had the right to bury my grandfather because he died on their ground. But most important still, they loved him as much as the Muslims loved him. And so that's where his grave remains.

I remembered journeying to the shrine with my mother. I must have been six or seven years old.

When we arrived we were received by dozens of people who lined the road. "Here they come, make way," people were saying. "Make way, these are his descendants." My mother and I were led to the shrine, which was covered with white sand and surrounded by slender trees. I remembered my mother kneeling on the sand and taking a handful of it, which she distributed amongst the people over and over again, until all those present had received sand from her. And then she prayed. Every day for more than two weeks, she repeated this ritual. We left the shrine with more than two dozen carriers whose sacks were filled with gifts the pilgrims had bestowed on us. My mother would always refer to that visit as one of the most memorable moments of her life.

I longed to visit her grave, but because she was buried in a nearby town, Koniyan, the townspeople asked me to wait until they were prepared to receive me. In the house allocated to me, I placed a few cousins in one room, a number of them in the other; all tested in the war, all prepared to protect me.

"Chief, I will sleep in the jeep in front of the house," the driver said. "No one will dare face me." My fear was eased, but I did not sleep that night out of excitement. I was thinking about my mother most of the time.

The next day, dozens crowded the road in Koniyan, singing a solemn song tinged with joy. I waited for the crowd, which moved at a snail's pace down the hill and up to where I had been asked to wait. The women fell over me with hugs, their hands moving clumsily across my sweaty face. A man edged his way through the throng of women and held my hands and would not let go until we reached the grave, which was located at the heart of the town. I thought I knew the man, and it turned out that he was another cousin – the son of an uncle who lived in Sierra Leone. As we arrived at the gravesite, the crowd left us behind.

The grass around the grave had been trimmed and a hedge of bamboo enclosed it. Standing there, I remembered my mother's shimmering dark skin; I recalled the sight of her, tall and dark, as she emerged from her house in colorful wrappers and with proud headgear to lead her apprentices to the local market where she reigned supreme. The Lomas, a people who had co-existed with us for centuries, had nicknamed her 'The Beautiful Mandingo'. Now she was no more.

One of the town elders asked me to say a few words. The words took shape in my mind but choked in my throat. The crowd burst into tears.

A town elder stood up. "Your mother's beauty was the envy of even the jinn's," he said. "Yes, her beauty was extraordinary. But even more than that, she was, as a human being, a replica of your grandfather. She was generous to a fault. Everything she ever earned she gave away. Let those who remember her contradict me."

I believed him.

Later, after the elders had said some prayers, the crowd led me to the town hall. It was there that I learned the true story of my mother's fate.

"A rebel commander caught your mother and pinned her to the ground," the town chief of Koniyan told me. "Believe me, Vali, for I was there when it happened. He fired a whole round at her but not a single bullet touched her. Yours is a unique family. It was not a bullet that killed your mother, but illness."

I chose not to believe him. In this anecdote, rendered so beautifully that even the most hardened skeptic would be inclined to believe it, lay the stark truth. My mother was killed by a rebel. In a tradition where truth took on many forms, I had been spared the pain of the hard truth by another, less painful truth.

In subsequent days, I learned to live with that truth. When not with the elders, whose stories almost always ended with a spark of wisdom, I would be in Wologizi, whiling away my time with childhood friends. Or I would be at the Kaihah River, where I had learned to swim. That part of the river which had once bustled with life was now shrouded in bushes. The first time I went to see it I had to cut my way to it with a machete. I remembered a tall tree from the top of which the best swimmers from the city would plunge into the river. I remembered lying in the sand with a book in hand after a swim, the world peaceful around me, the story and the world merging into one, the story becoming my story. Places like the banks of that river had formed me, so that even now, after having been away for more than two decades, my memories keep bringing me back to it, to the scent of the trees, to the touch of the sand, to the voices of girls rising with laughter as we chased them along the sandy banks, to the smell of the earth, to the overcrowded home, to the place where I first saw daylight.

Childhood friends, whose faces I recognized but whose names I had forgotten, poured daily into the compound to share the past with me. Their war experiences varied: some had been forced to fight, others had stood up to the rebels. And most of them had fled the war to Guinea or Sierra Leone, or had sought refuge in the forest surrounding Wologizi until the war was over.

"When we returned to Wologizi, we met a place that had turned into bush," one of them told me. "Yes, we hunted deer and opossums right where we are now sitting."

The war made some wealthy, while others who had once been rich lost everything. The effect was so profound that, whenever I walked the streets of Wologizi, I could see that places where once the homes of the wealthy had stood were now empty, while those who had taken up the places of the wealthy were mostly strangers to me. Some of my friends, whom many had once thought would amount to nothing in life, now belonged to the wealthy group. The war had come and gone, reversing fortunes and leaving frustrations and unsettled scores in its wake.

The longer I stayed in Wologizi, commuting every day to Koniyan, the more I longed to return to Belgium, to the ritual of waking up in the early hours to leave for work and stand along an assembly line, feeling the hard metal, arranging parts, and then, finally, seeing the finished product, a huge truck, painted and polished, driving out of the colossal building for a test ride.

I finally left Wologizi early one morning, my brother Sekou and some of the cousins accompanying me. We had been driving for hours when we saw a man standing alongside the road, waving at our car, asking for a lift. I asked the driver to stop, for we still had space for one person. When we drew up to the man, my brother said, as if he'd seen a ghost, "Drive on, drive on quickly."

His reaction baffled me. "What was the matter?"

Sekou was suddenly sweating, and he swept his face with his hand. "He was the man who held our mother at gunpoint in Koniyan and tried to kill her. Yes, he was the one who shot at our mother! I can never forget that face. I was there! He's the one."

The driver sucked his teeth. "Chief, let me handle this," he said. Before I could say anything, he had turned the car around and was speeding toward the man.

"Wait, wait, don't do anything yet," I said. I could not believe that I had found my mother's murderer! But the driver jumped from the car and was upon the man. He held him by the collar and dragged him to my brother.

"Do you remember this man?" the driver asked, spitting in his face. "Do you remember him?"

The man burst into tears. "I've never seen this man before, Chief," he said, looking at me standing a distance away, too stunned to react. "Why are you treating me like this?"

Sekou then recounted the incident with a tremor in his voice. "You shot our mother. Remember, the bullets were deflected, but you intended to kill her. Yes, you intended to kill her!"

"Kill an innocent woman?" protested the man. "I was never involved in the war."

The driver slapped him, but the man remained adamant. He was a skinny man in a worn-out shirt and trousers, his shoes patched all over – a destitute in fact.

My brother shook his head. "I could not forget your face even after a hundred years. You were the one who wanted to kill our mother. We were fleeing to Sierra Leone and we were in Koniyan. You took our property, including my watch, the jewelry, and some other goods. You were the one who stripped me of my clothes and left me standing naked. I cannot forget your face. You were the one who shot at our mother."

Why was my brother still insisting that our mother had survived a gunshot? I approached the man. He was trembling now, and with every step I took towards him, he withdrew into himself. At the point when I was so close to him that I could smell his fear, the man fell to his knees and held my feet. "Don't kill me, Chief. I was never part of the war. Never killed a human being, let alone a woman."

Then I heard my brother say, his voice sounding distant, out of this world: "Killing him will not bring back our mother. Let him be. The war is over."

I turned to him. A sudden wind seemed to have risen, and a cold swept across my body. "So you are telling me that he did kill our mother?"

My brother shook his head. "I am telling you that our mother has passed on. Whatever you do cannot bring her back."

The driver sucked his teeth. "Even if we don't kill him, Chief, at least let us break his arms and legs," he said. "He deserves it."

But I had become paralyzed. A deep, chilly silence seemed to have descended on me, a strange cold beneath the sweat and the heat around me. It was as if I had landed in a dream in which the action was beyond my control. The man was sobbing now, his hold on my feet stronger. It was my brother who led me to the car. When I turned around, I saw that the man had not left his kneeling position.

"I swear he was the one," Sekou said as he recounted the incident to our elder brother Edmond that night. The latter shook his head and kept silent. By then the driver had gone home, and once again the city had been plunged into a ceaseless round of church songs and drums that would go on all night long. The cold that had taken hold of me settled deep.

Vamba Sherif

There are many stories about homecoming, about writers returning home, about exile and its effect on people. The most famous is of course *The Odyssey of Homer*, but we also have stories like *A Dream of Africa* by Laye Kamara, *A State of Independence* by Caryl Phillips, and many others. This story was inspired by my visit to Liberia after the war. I wanted to reflect on homecoming, on the lives lived in my absence, on nostalgia and how we long to fix the past, to rescue it from oblivion.

I was away during the war, living in Kuwait and later in Syria and then The Netherlands. I was not directly affected by war, but I was a victim of the war, like many other Liberians. Every day, I saw images of the war in Liberia, graphic and horrible images. I was anxious to return to Liberia and see what war had done to the country. The loss of lives, including those close to me, profoundly affected my life and writings in The Netherlands.

In my story I want to convey the sense of loss, the need to belong and not really belonging to the world left behind, and the world of the adopted country. *Homecoming* is as relevant today as it was yesterday. Except that the war is behind us now, and we are heading toward the future. I've learned a lot about life since writing the story. I've learned to live with the losses from the Liberian civil war and to focus on the future. But I keep remembering the past. May we all remember what happened in the war and learn from it.

About the Contributors

M. Woryonwon Roberts has been a street peddler, shopkeeper, sports director and classroom teacher. He is a practitioner and facilitator of *Reading and Writing for Critical Thinking (RWCT)*, and has run RWCT trainings for educators across Liberia and in Zambia, Malawi and Sierra Leone. Roberts currently works as a teacher educator and textbook writer.

Gii-Hne S. Russell was born in the town of Bong Mines, in Bong County, and studied Library Science at Stella Maris Polytechnic. He is the author of three children's books, and has poems and a short story published in *A Day Under the Palaver Hut*—an anthology by Critical Thinking Liberia (CT-L).

Vamba Sherif was born in Liberia and spent parts of his youth in Kuwait where he completed his secondary schooling. He fled the First Gulf War and settled in Syria, and then in The Netherlands where he read Law. His novels include *Land of My Fathers, Bound to Secrecy* and *The Black Napoleon*. His work has been translated into many languages. Sherif reviews music and films, and collects rare books on Africa.

Augustus Y. Voahn was born in Zuolay, Nimba County, in the northeastern region of Liberia. He has a B.Sc. in Social Work from the Mother Patern College of Health Sciences, and has worked in many rural communities in Liberia. His areas of involvement include community development, child protection, women's empowerment and girls' education. Voahn is the author of three books for children—*Under the Bridge, Swimming at Ten,* and *Uncle Jallah Will Fix It.*

Elma Shaw experienced a coup d'état in Liberia that set her on a path to explore and write about issues of peace and justice. Her award-winning novel, *Redemption Road*, inspired a documentary about female fighters who survived the civil war that began in 1989. Shaw has written articles for *Sea Breeze Journal of Contemporary Liberian Writings, Liberia Travel & Life Magazine, Pambazuka News, UNMIL Focus,* and other publications. A long-time champion for women and girls, she supports girls' education, and recently worked with The What To Expect Foundation as lead writer for the *Big Belly Business* pregnancy guide. Shaw currently lives in Rwanda, where she is working on a new book and helping Africa's game changers become authors too.

Also by Cotton Tree Press

Can a country man make it in Liberia? This is the question Sumowor Gbamokorli wrestles with during his long, eventful journey from village life to the capital city, where *kwii* men seem to have all the power. Will he be able to escape the webs of tribal and "civilized" societies that both deny him the freedom to live up to his ambitions?

Set in the mid-1960s, *Birds Are Singing* gives us a glimpse into rituals of secret societies and traditions from rural Liberia, and into the nature of unscrupulous folk that rule in the city. Through all the temptations, will Korli stay true to himself and to his wife, Leanya? Will he ever be accepted for his talents and respected for his vision? Can a man like Korli make it in Liberia?

We invite you to turn the page for an excerpt from this exciting novel.

BIRDS ARE SINGING

BY WILTON SANKAWULO

PROLOGUE

When the man he had known all his life as his father told him at midnight that, in fact, he wasn't his father, Sumowor Vakpeeh Gbamokorli had lain stunned on his sleeping mat by the fireside, staring at the black rafter ceiling until the last glow of embers died and roosters declared dawn. Old Man Nuulaa had shaken him by the shoulder until he awoke, yawned, shoved the bedclothes down to his waist, and looked at him with squinting eyes.

"Yes, Data?" he drawled and rubbed the sleep from his eyes, still yawning.

Bending over him, Nuulaa whispered, "I have something very important to tell you. Come with me." Unbolting the coarse wooden door quietly, Nuulaa stepped onto the porch, which was fenced with wattle to keep off goats and sheep.

Korli sobered, his heart beat faster, he inhaled the musty air deeply and expelled it slowly. Sitting up with an effort and wrapping his arms around his knees, he wondered what errand his demanding Old Man had contrived for him so late in the night. Man-to-man talk usually occurred in a *Kpaan* on the outskirts of town, or on a hunting or fishing excursion. The tidings his father had for him must be ominous since they couldn't wait for day to break. Korli hoped they weren't another invitation for him to join *Gborlorkpilii*, a society he despised. Obviously testing his resolve, Nuulaa repeatedly urged him to join the water society as they hunted, fished, or worked on the farm, but Korli always expressed only his contempt for it.

"Membership in the Poro and snake societies is enough for me, Data," he'd tell him. Elaborating the obvious, he'd explain that the Poro taught him how to subdue the jungle with its fiendish creatures to make a living, and that the snake society taught him how to protect himself against snakebite and the curatives to treat it were he bitten. He'd add, to Nuulaa's disgust, "Data, the other societies are mere diversions and a menace. Any man who values his life won't bother with them."

Nuulaa usually took his stubborn and almost impertinent reply in stride but not without a bit of warning:

"Since you're a full-fledged *kenamu*, it's true you don't need to join the minor societies," he'd start on an encouraging note. "However, our ancestors passed them to us for our protection. You enjoy their blessings and benefit from the fellowship and confidence of men when you join them. The spirit and *gbon* societies, for example, give you power over spirits and witches, respectively. The leopard society makes leopards harmless when you confront them, and the sheep society makes you brave. The water society is especially important, for wherever you go, you'll meet creeks and rivers. Once you become a member of it, you'll have power over all water creatures. Besides these benefits, there's nothing like the fellowship you enjoy as a member of these societies. Son, you can't go through life alone however wise, rich, or powerful you may be."

Korli always had ready rejoinders for the argument, but in deference to his Poro training, he'd let his father have the last word. You don't argue with your senior, especially your parent. He decided, however, to make a clean breast of his resentment of the despicable society should his father raise the subject tonight. He was tired of it; it was making him feel like an alien.

Wrapped in thick homespun bedclothes to ward off December's biting cold, they sat facing each other in rattan chairs on the porch. Except for the screeching of crickets, the flickering lights of fireflies, and the perpetual roaring of the Deyn River, the night was utterly dark and quiet. Not a trace of moon- or starlight showed in the sky, and the silence was profound.

"You're now a man, a seasoned *kenamu*, ready for weighty news," the Old Man murmured almost inaudibly in Korli's attentive ears to prepare him for the grim message. But this initial remark only increased Korli's agitation.

His heart had bubbled with joy and pride when his father called him a man at so young an age—he was only eighteen—and appealed to his confidence, but the unusual setting of the secret talk and the solemn tone of his voice dispersed the ecstasy. After a long pause, Nuulaa drew a deep sigh and, looking at Korli's dim profile, said:

"I forbid you to cry or grieve over what I'm about to tell you. Now that you'll soon face the world on your own, I must confront you with these sad tidings to spare you unexplained sickness, accident, or sudden death. Crocodile killed your father while your mother was pregnant with you, and your mother died while giving you birth. Felenkpeh and I took you as our child after your parents' death, so I'm really your uncle." Nuulaa paused, stared briefly at the grisly night, and quickly wrapped up his message: "We're still your parents, however, and this house is still your home. According to our custom, the rightful father of a child is its uncle, anyway, and a woman is mother to every child. You have all our blessings, Korli. May God and the ancestors protect, prosper, and grant you long life." Then Nuulaa rushed into the house to avoid any questions Korli might have, leaving him to wrestle alone with the perplexing revelation.

* * *

Nuulaa Gbunakpele Bharsi was a man of discipline and industry, virtues he instilled in his three sons, two of whom had married at a young age and left the home. Mothers were responsible for the upbringing of girls, but Nuulaa always reminded his only daughter Moima, whenever she neglected her duties, that discipline was as important for a woman as for a man. He was proud of rearing his children according to the best of Kpelle traditions. Except for Korli, who had a mind and plan of his own—he wondered how he had come by such attitude—the boys followed his footsteps. With time, he hoped Korli would grasp his vision as his brothers had done.

Nuulaa had been born premature and beset with every conceivable childhood illness. His mother, the fifth wife of his father, Bhalasia, had three children but only he and one of two sisters had survived. Bhalasia, whose hands were full with the many responsibilities of his large family—he fathered more than fifty children—did not care for his mother and her children as he should have done, undoubtedly because she was the youngest of his wives. Nobody expected Nuulaa to live, for sickness crushed him constantly during most of his childhood days. His mother went virtually naked by pawning her clothes to pay legions of *Zoes* to teach her which herbs to use to treat him. At the age of five, Nuulaa still rode his mother's back to and from the farm because he was too weak to walk. Then one day he had insisted on walking to the farm on his own feet. It was a slow and tedious journey, but as of that day, he could walk as freely as his peers and even do petty chores on the farm. People said that his sudden and unexpected recovery was a miracle. Having studied the herbs his mother used to treat him, Nuulaa treated sick children as a child. As a grown man, he could join broken bones, cure insanity, and drive spirits and witches from people—powers, he said, his ancestors had given him in dreams. His fame spread throughout Fuama Chiefdom, much to everybody's surprise, for he was never a Zoe apprentice, nor was any member of his family ever a Zoe. When the Chief Poro Zoe of Fuama Chiefdom died, the Land—the tribe and all its leaders, past and present—appointed him as his successor. Under his leadership, Poro initiations flourished and the Land was secure and fruitful.

* * *

Originally cattle breeders, shepherds, and goat herders, the Kpelle had fled with their animals to the fertile rainforest in the west away from the eastern world where drought had killed every plant, and great winds had built enormous sand domes all over the land. They fought many hostile tribesmen *en route* to the forest region, losing hundreds of warriors and half their animals. They finally settled in Fuama, an evergreen forest replete with flora and fauna.

Fuama Chiefdom became a bone of contention when they began exploiting its fallow farmlands, herds of animals, and swarms of fishes. The Bassa from the east and the Gola from the south conquered it in succession, enslaved half the people and looted their possessions, but the people repossessed the land after many battles. The last wave of invaders comprised the wealthy Gbandi Chief Zolu Doma of Tahama Chiefdom near the Guinean border. He had fled with a large entourage from a raging war Guinean tribesman had waged on Gbandi- and Lomaland. Chief Doma had more than a hundred wives, thousands of cattle, countless warriors, man- and maidservants, and numerous bags of iron money. He could have conquered Fuama Chiefdom by force had he wished, for he came from a long line of brave warriors, such as Seimavile Halingi who offered himself as a living sacrifice to save his people from Wono giants in what is now Wubomai. But the old Chief discovered that love was the most potent weapon of conquest. He shared his cattle, money, and virgins with the Land and appealed to them for a sitting place. When Chief Kpakila Dwalu died, the Land made him his successor. They turned Fuama Chiefdom over to him with white kola and permitted him to settle wherever he liked. In a generation, Kpelle culture absorbed Chief Doma and his people; their origin no longer mattered to the people. Although his rule was brief, it made a lasting impact on the Land. The son who succeeded him was not as generous or gifted in leadership as his father had been. The only advantage he brought to the chieftaincy was his father's name and reputation, but he had a firm grip on the Land because the name "Doma" meant something in Fuama in those early days. The people endured him until a new president took the Chair in Liberia and decreed that tribal people elect their Chiefs. It wasn't customary with the people to contest leadership, but they did it, if only to put their own flesh and blood on the Stool again. Who else could be their candidate but the Chief of the Poro Zoes of Fuama Chiefdom?

To ensure victory, Zoe Nuulaa decided to sacrifice his most beloved son to the river goddess as other candidates were doing. Only Korli qualified for the supreme sacrifice. He was ambitious like his father, handsome, strong, reserved, and uncorrupted by the recklessness of youth such as chasing wild women, drinking strong drinks excessively, or devoting too much time to festivals. He enjoyed the love and respect of his family and was the pride of the Land. Everybody believed that he was destined for greatness.

Informing Felenkpeh about his decision was a duty Nuulaa preferred not to perform if he had a choice in the matter. Tradition required that both parents of a sacrificial victim give their consent before the victim was killed, or the sacrifice would not yield the desired result. Delivering the deadly blow to Felenkpeh was no problem, of course. Had he not dealt out death sentences to many a violator of Poro laws? But Zoe Nuulaa did not want to risk having Felenkpeh break down under the weight of the blow and consequently expose the secret. It'd mean her execution with Korli and a defamation of the family's name for all time. He consulted the Council of Poro Zoes on the matter. They recommended that three representatives of the Council of Sande Zoes deliver the blow. After giving the matter some thought, he refused to involve other people in what he perceived as a personal affair. Who would vote for a leader that could not carry out his own decision?

Before dawn one morning, Nuulaa told Felenkpeh about the planned ordeal with three white kola nuts. Felenkpeh had fainted, her body awash with perspiration. Zoe Nuulaa found himself confronted with the worst dilemma of his life. The creature he loved most was on the point of death! Forgetting his pride, he appealed to the Sande Zoes of Haindi for help. They took Felenkpeh's limp body to a sacred grove and poured water on her until she came to. Then, they bade her to honor her Sande oath by bearing the tragic news with courage on behalf of women. Her very life belonged to the Land, not to speak of those of her children. Felenkpeh had requested that she visit her mother before making a decision. When the women informed Nuulaa about her request, he did not only approve of it, he told her that he had, in fact, abandoned the sacrifice. He'd win the election by virtue of merit. Was he not the custodian of the traditions and life of the Land? He told his wife to take Korli with her and spend all the time she wanted at home, but Korli had insisted on remaining to help run his father's campaign. His father's victory, he thought, would give him an opportunity to become a Chief someday. Felenkpeh had spent a month in Gboryoimu and returned to find Korli in good health. She did not know that Zoe Nuulaa had planned a fantastic strategy to capture Korli for the sacrifice.

To read the rest of *Birds Are Singing*, visit your favorite online retailer or bookstore to purchase or order a copy. You may also visit our website at www.ctpbooks.com to learn more about our work, and sign up for updates. To order discounted copies of any of our books in bulk for your institution, organization or charity, please contact the publisher at CottonTreePress@gmail.com

Praise for Birds Are Singing

"*Birds Are Singing* holds a mirror up to Liberia and reveals a place where the best and brightest are cut down time and time again to the detriment of all. And we—Liberian people—must read it with that same urgency with which Sankawulo put it down as the ultimate deadline loomed before him. And then read it again...until we see our face(s), hear our voice(s) and those of our ancestors, settlers and indigenous alike, as they really are. Maybe then we'll break the curse we would all like to pretend does not exist."

—Sengbe Kona Khasu
Musician, Screenwriter and Director
Hunting in America and We Want Election, No More Selection: A Documentary on the Liberian Election of 2005

"*Birds Are Singing* gives great insight into Liberian history, culture and politics. Like Sankawulo's previous novels, *The Rain and the Night*, and *Sundown at Dawn*, it confirms his brilliant role as a teacher, historian and preserver of culture. Birds Are Singing not only imparts to the reader his knowledge of Liberia's past, but it also lays out, in Korli's parable, the need to analyze past failures to rectify them and chart a successful future as individuals and as a nation."

—Althea Romeo-Mark
author of *If Only the Dust Would Settle: Selected Poems*

"Sankawulo's last song is his richest, deepest, most fearless plumbing of the insistent themes he explored throughout his writing life…. No one—whether rural or urban—is spared Sankawulo's hawk-eyed gaze. Monrovia of the Tubman years teems with cutthroats, backstabbers, con artists, swindlers, and ruthless social climbers. Traditional moorings are threatened by urban anonymity. The natural beauty of Haindi and its environs is set against the stronghold of both empowering and corrosive traditions. This book is Sankawulo's *magnum opus*, his final compulsive effort to be heard and understood, his vision of a just, egalitarian, productive Liberian society, his thorough understanding of both our better natures and our very ugly, wicked ways, and his prayer for our redemption."

—Stephanie Horton
Sea Breeze Journal of Contemporary Liberian Writings

www.ingramcontent.com/pod-product-compliance
Lightning Source LLC
Chambersburg PA
CBHW030654110726
47901CB00002B/713